W9-DBX-867
6437
HARRIS COUNTY PUBLIC LIBRARY

THE CITY ON THE OTHER SIDE

THE CITY ON THE OTHER SIDE

MAIRGHREAD SCOTT

ROBIN ROBINSON

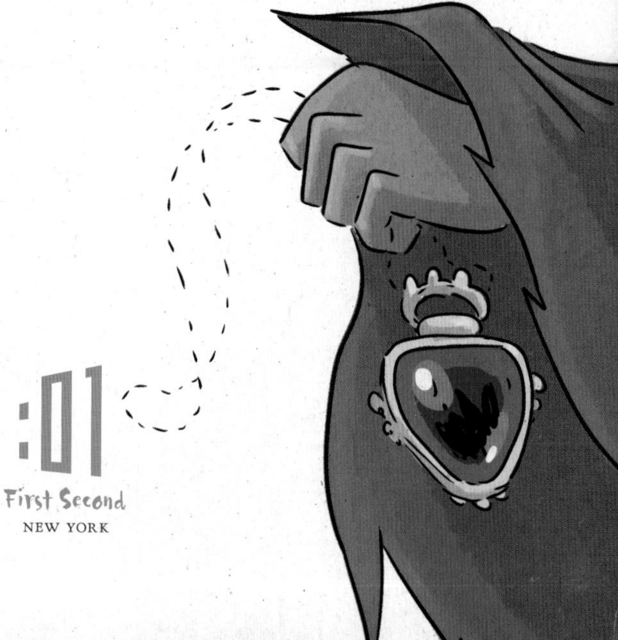

:01
First Second
NEW YORK

Once upon a time, there was a kingdom of fairies called the *Seelie.*
Bright and shining, these fairies touched every aspect of our world.

They blessed fern and bird and human beings alike.

But there was another kingdom of fairies. One whose job it was to bless worm and stone and crumbling log.

They were called the *Unseelie.*

Many conflicts arose between them. But even though they had been at peace for centuries, these two kingdoms...

...were, again, at war.

The Unseelie were led by the dreaded Prince Coscar.
My lord!
There's no sign of Ro'hish.

The old coward's hiding. Breach the castle!

I *will* have back what he stole from me, even if I must soak the ground in blood to do it.

Onward! For glory!

--it is not about dishonor, my lord. It--
King Ro'hish!

Our walls are breached. Unseelie are inside the castle!

You must go now, my lord!
This is one of the last Seelie forts in this area. If we lose it *and* you, the war is over.
Your concern touches my heart, dear friends.

But much of my power has already passed to my daughter. *She* is the key to defeating Coscar. Not I.
There is no word from Id'naress, Your Highness.
We can't even be sure she's alive.

Id'naress lives. And Miyori will find her.
Pista, you are my fastest messenger, so this terrible task must fall to you.
You must deliver *this* to Miyori. He is still in the city.

What is it, my king?
It is a weapon of Coscar's own design. An object of tremendous power.

Miyori must get this weapon to Id'naress. With it, she may yet be able to break Prince Coscar.
And Coscar must break if this war is to end. Now go!

You could come with me, my king. You would survive.
No. There is still much to do.

There is nothing more important to the Seelie than honor.
And no Seelie feels the weight of that honor more than their king, their leader.
It is the leader's duty to keep their people free.
It is their duty to keep their people safe.
No matter the cost.

Yield!

Your Highness!
I said "yield," Koron.

HOLD!
We will not strike surrendering forces.
Tell Coscar we need him at the front.

Thank you. That was--
What are your terms, Ro'hish?
I ask only that you spare the lives of my followers.
Fine. Allow me to confer with my master.

You do not have to do this, Your Highness.
Silence.

Ro'hish. It has been too long.

I was just discussing my terms of surrender with your captain, Coscar. If you spare my people, then my castle, and my life, are yours.

If you wish your people spared, Ro'hish, you'll return what was taken from me.
My necklace for *their* lives.

Oh, Coscar.
You ask for the one thing you will never have.
"The necklace is already gone."
And you will never see it again until you release my daughter from wherever you imprisoned her!
Lies! Your daughter abandoned her--

KRRCK

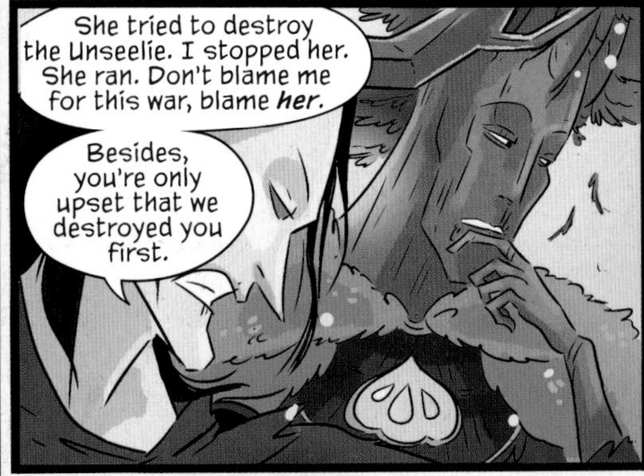
She tried to destroy the Unseelie. I stopped her. She ran. Don't blame me for this war, blame *her*.
Besides, you're only upset that we destroyed you first.

Id'naress is not some innocent prisoner. She is in hiding, pretending to be a martyr even as she protects her own skin.

Spine! Gather my scouts and find the necklace. It can't be far.

Yes, sir. But what of the prisoners?
I have no necklace. There will be no prisoners.

But, Coscar, we've won.
Are you questioning my orders? After all I've done for you? For *our* people?

Do you think you cannot be replaced?
No, sir. It will be done.
See that it is. I'm returning to the city as soon as this place is purged. Bring the necklace to me there.

You heard him!
FAN OUT!

War and pain raged in the world of Fairy.
On both sides.

But the fairy world is not the only world. The human world continued...
THM
...unaware of the war that was destroying them as well.

Quickly, ladies. Madam is already at table.

Not that she eats anything.
Abigail! That is not your place to say.
HEAT WAVE SPURS CRIME WAVE

COLUMBUS
FORT MASON
O DE YOUNG MUSEUM
TOURING SCULPTURE
CALIFORNIA
STREET
PORTRERO
WALL
TASTE OF CANTON
ITALIA
DE YOUNG MUSEUM
TWIN PEAKS
REBUILDING
COAT BLVD

Isabel!

Mother?
A woman of breeding is never late to breakfast.

Especially not on her mother's last day before her trip. I'll be relieved to have some distance between me and this filthy city.
I like the city.

Nonsense! Europe is the place to see, and I will take you along with me someday.
I don't want to see Europe; I want to see the city here.
You see it all the time, when Charles takes you to your tutors.

I don't let you wander through the rubble and I won't apologize for wanting my daughter clean and well-cared for.
RIME
POLICE HAVE SUSPECT
REPORT
CITY FLOUNDERING
LOST CHILDREN?

I don't like Europe.
Everyone loves Europe, ***mi hija.****
*my daughter

Next year, of course, you'll be able to go to summer camp.
I don't like camp, either.

Tontería!* You'll love camp.
I could stay here while you're gone. Charles could watch me.
*Nonsense

And what kind of mother would that make me, abandoning my daughter in a place like this?

Second-rate culture.
Vagabonds everywhere.
More smog than fog.
You, young lady, see too much of this place as it is.

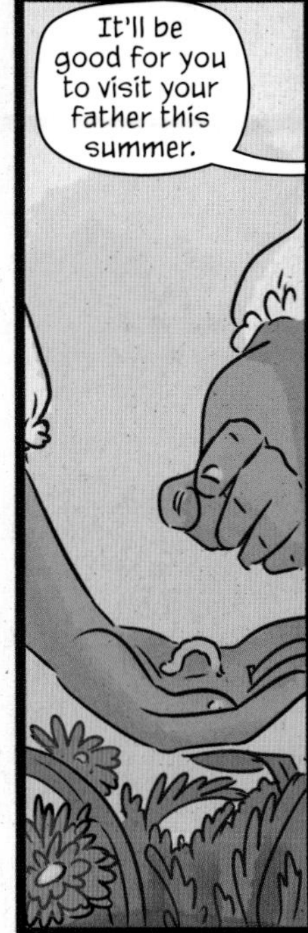

Charles! Shouldn't you be leaving? We can't dawdle all day.
Yes, ma'am.

Have fun, ***mi hija.***
Yes, ma'am.

At least one of us gets to stay.

Come along, miss.

Your father is quite the sculptor, miss. I'm sure you'll learn a great deal from him.

And you haven't been to Carmel in so long it's practically a new place. How exciting!

Mother doesn't like me to get dirty. I remember there being lots of dirt in the country, right?

Perhaps. But you never know what's around a corner until you take the turn.

Thank you, Charles.
All part of the job, miss.

I'm sure your father will be delighted to meet--umm--**see** you again.
Is it much farther?
A bit, miss.
Here we are!

Are these...Father's sculptures?
I would assume so.

I'm not sure where your father is, though.
KNCK
KNCK
KNCK

...I'll try to locate him.
I'll just stay here. Try not to get dirty.

Ah-hem.
Hello?!

Is anyone here?

CHNK!
TNK!
Oh!

Sir?
Sir!
Charles! It's been too long.
What brings you all the way out here?
Sir, I contacted you several weeks ago...
Of course! Isabel! Ah! Things have been so crazy, I can't keep track of my own name!

*Princesa!** How is my little girl?
Hello... Father. How are you?
Please! It's Papa! So formal, this one.
*Princess

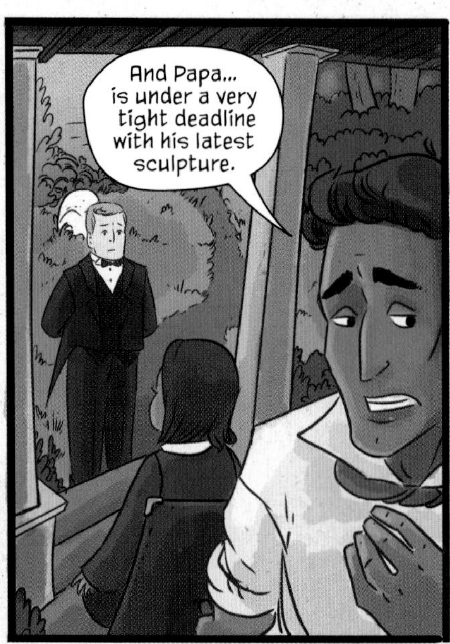
And Papa... is under a very tight deadline with his latest sculpture.

But, of course, an independent little girl like you can amuse yourself while I work.
I suppose.

Give my love to Rosalia, Charles. We'll handle things from here.
Good-bye, Charles.

Your room is *mostly* set up. It just needs a little elbow grease.

What do you think?

Not as spotless as your *mother* would want, but we don't have to tell her, do we?

No, Papa.
Fear not, princesa. I'll be back as soon as I finish one last step. Minutes only, I promise.
You don't need to lift a finger.

Rwr.
Hi there. Do you live here on your own?

Come here, ***peluche.****
*a stuffed animal

pss pss pss

Nonono!
Rarrr

Shoo. You can't eat flowers.

Oh, no! I'm sorry! I didn't mean to get...

...dirty.
Hmm.

Let's get you a little more light.

You must be thirsty.

Don't worry. I know mushrooms like a bit more shade.

And we're almost done.
grrgle
Huh?

And now... supper.

SPLSH
SHHSH

errh...

Charles said get the pan hot first, then--

Princesa!

What are you doing? I said I'd be right back.
I was just making eggs.
That is for Papa to do.

Here. We can't have a princesa getting burnt fingers on her first day here, can we?
No, Papa.

See, princesa? Papa has everything under control.

But, he does need his princesa's help with one thing.

Papa must get back to work and he needs you to be a big girl and put yourself to bed.
But it's not even dark yet.

KRCH!
SHHK SHHHK
Papa?

Hello?
Is someone there?
Kitty? Are you okay?
tchh tchh
Ki..,ma... run...
Gah!

How...how do you see me? Why am I on this side of the Veil?
I don't-- Are you okay?

No. The Unseelie... They are coming.

I'm sorry. I don't know what that means.

Are you hurt--?

What's happening? I can't move my hand!
It's the necklace. I--I'm not sure what's going on.

Where are we?

The necklace... It pulled us back to my side of the Veil. We're in the realm of the fairies.

I-- Is that my house?

A Seelie messenger?!
We can't face Unseelie. Not on our own!
Not for long. Looks like Unseelie.
Now they're attacking messengers?
You're all... fairies?

My lady, are you okay?
No. But a pack of Unseelie scouts is on its way.
We do not have ti--
FFPT
Fire! Fire on them all!
Come on, you overgrown squeeze-box scoundrels!
Don't listen to that crazy fungus! We have to get out of here!

Whoever they are, I wish they'd go away.
Stay back! This is Unseelie business!

Ahh!

Retreat!

What's going on?!
I don't know...I have never seen this type of magic before.
Whatever it is, keep doing it!

Fall back! Run!

You did it, human!
You'll be playin' a different tune when Ro'hish gets his hands on you!

I'm sorry.
Don't be. You did a brave thing, child.

We have to get you to a doctor!
No. It is too late for me, but not for my--ah--mission.

What... is your name?
Isabel.

Isabel...It means "God is my oath." I need you to make an oath to me now, Isabel.

Yes. Anything.
Do not be so eager. It is unfair of me to ask it at all.

But the necklace responds to you. It must mean something...

This necklace must go to the Seelie general, Miyori.
No! Please stay awake.
He is in the city, but I know not... where.

He must have it. Everything... Everything depends on it.
Swear... that... you...

I promise.

...I just...don't know who Miyori is.
Pfft! Well, stick close to Ol' Button, kiddo.

Ol' Button? More like Old Loudmouth.
heheheheh
You just jumped into the deep end, feet first.
Wait! We're helping? Why are we helping? I don't think we should get involved.

We're just telling her what's going on.
But what if...Coscar... finds out we helped?

Who's Coscar?
One nasty guy, spriteling.
An antlered, grasping, know-nothing monolith. That's what he is.

"There are two types of fairies in our kingdom, the Seelie and the Unseelie.
"Unlike human kingdoms, fairies switch who's in control. Each court has a monarch who rules for half the year.
"For us, that's Id'naress and Coscar.
"Now, each court is supposedly equal. But *we're* all Seelie here.
"And Unseelie are pointy, slimy, and don't play well with others...especially not humans.
"This isn't the first Cold Iron War.
"That's what it's called when fairy fights fairy.
"But it could be the last.
"Coscar decided he didn't want to share power with humans, or the Seelie, or anybody else.
"He kidnapped Id'naress, hid her away, and stole her power.

"Coscar declared himself to be king and the Unseelie to be in charge forever.
"King Ro'hish is fighting, but he gave up most of his power to Id'naress, and Coscar's been more powerful than anyone expected.
"The city's completely under Coscar's control. Everyone lives by his laws.
"And every day he takes more of the forest as well."
"How long has Id'naress been missing?"
"Don't you remember it?
"It was the day your city burned."

Coscar caused the earthquake? But that was in my world!
Our worlds aren't separate, spriteling.
There's barely a grass blade's width of magic between them.
We call it the Veil.
But just because it separates us doesn't mean we don't affect each other.
A war on our side makes the earth jiggle like jelly on your side. A building built on your side gives us itchy roots.

So if Coscar wins, the city could be destroyed all over again!

Possibly. Coscar doesn't like humans. If he gains complete control over our realm, he may wage war on yours next.
All the more reason to grab our spores and go!

A Seelie messenger puffed out her last breath to say knobby knees here has gotta get this necklace to the city, and I intend to make sure she does it! Who's with me?!
...I don't know how we can help.

Help?! I lived in the city. I know it like the back of my hand.

I *served* in the army.
A reeeaaal long time ago.
I'd take the dang thing myself except...well, when a necklace does more than look pretty, I've found it's best to leave it be.

And since no one *else* is volunteering...

Miss, you just follow Button. I'll get you to where you need go.

But you don't have to. You're still very young. You don't need to go.

I...

Of course she'll do it. She swore to!
She's just a child. She can't go traipsing off to the city. Her parents will worry!
No one's going to worry about me. No one notices anything I do.

At least not in *my* world.

I'm going to the city.
A-***HA!*** What did I tell you? She's a true warrior! Practically a Seelie herself!

Onward!
Um...Mr. Button? Do we have time for me to pack a few things first?

Right! But make it quick; we have a couple of worlds to save.

Don't worry about these clothes. Mother says they aren't pretty anymore.
Probably don't want to eat me. But I say you can never go wrong with a flashlight.
I've already got a map of the city, but you need snacks on an adventure!
Do we need rope? Who am I kidding, you always need rope.
I guess... Why is there rope in the living room?
You're his offspring, not me.
Actually I should probably grab a little mulch, too. A nice mulch does wonders for everyone.

Hurry up, Izzy. The sooner we bag that Unseelie menace the sooner you can get back to your dad.

Of course... when I come back.

Sooo tiiired...

Where is the necklace? The messenger?!
My lady, we killed the messenger but don't have the necklace.

What?! Coscar ordered the necklace be returned!
It wasn't our fault!
Pfft
There was a magic girl, a human. She drove us away and stole the necklace!

Humans aren't magic! That's the whole point of them!
She was! And she was on this side of the Veil! She used the necklace!

A human with magic? That can only be trouble.
What did she look like?

Uhhh... human?
Yes! Very human. Two eyes, a mouth, everything.

THEY ALL HAVE THOSE!

She was short...shorter than me. Her hair and skin were brown. And her petals were blue.
And you'd recognize her, if you saw her again?

Uhhh...
Of course, captain.
Tell me your name, soldier.
Torrent, ma'am.

Well, Torrent. Today you get a chance to prove yourself. Coscar wants this necklace.

We will find this thief and bring back the prince's treasure...or rend the world trying.

Button...
Do all fairies hate humans?
Humans? I don't really consider 'em much myself. Your dad's okay. But it wouldn't kill him to water our garden now and then.
But you said Coscar hates humans. Why?
Because Id'naress ***doesn't.*** Humans love to change the world, but sometimes fairies get hurt in the process.
Fairies like Coscar think humans are the enemy. They wanted to fight.
But Id'naress thinks that we should work with Humanity.
As your power grew, her power grew.
And Coscar's power?
It...didn't.
I think Coscar was scared, and nothing's more dangerous than fear.

So that's why he made the earthquake.

"I don't remember the Great Quake exactly.
"What I remember is *fire.*
"It raged for days.
"...I can still smell it sometimes."

Hey...
You with
me?

That quake
hurt us, too, kiddo.
No Seelie worth
their skin'll let him
do that again.

And with me on
the case, Coscar's gonna
be out of commission
before he can even think
about it.
With
your help, of
course.

After all,
you've got
longer
legs.

We don't
wanna miss
our train.

Where are we?
Carmel.
Haven't you ever been? It's the sweetest city by the sea.
On the ***human*** side of the Veil. But it doesn't look like this.
Well, stick close and keep your head down. Try not to attract any attention.
Don't mind my niece. Her petals are just a little wilted today.

Don't stare. You're already drawing people's notice as it is, looking so... human.
I mean, if you were purple it'd be something, but...
I *am* human.

I can't help what I look like.
Trust me, I know.

I think I recognize the store across the way. There was a store like it in *my* Carmel.

GENERAL STO

But even though it's in the same place, it's not here in the same way. Does that make sense?

As much sense as humans ever make. Stay here and sit tight. I'll scout out the train station.

Unseelie jerks.

...Okay... huff...there's good news and bad news.
What's the good news?
Well, they haven't completely locked down the station and we're not currently in jail.

Mop.

Basket.

Two cans of peaches.

Spiderwebs.

Mop.

How do I look?

Basket.

Spiderwebs.

Decidedly odd, so we'd better get movin'.

Two cans of peaches.

Hey, you! Stop!

You don't want to lose your peaches. Right?
Sure wouldn't, sir.

Toldja.
Just take a seat and don't let that necklace do anything weird.

Now we just need to sit tight until we get there.

Isabel?
ISABEL!
I'll be right back. I'm just looking for the restroom.
It's in the other direction.

Well, that's what he *claims.*

Just try it, sweetie. You'll like it.

Morning, little...um... lady. Anything take your fancy?

Hmmm... not sure.

Do you have anything with jam?

POP!

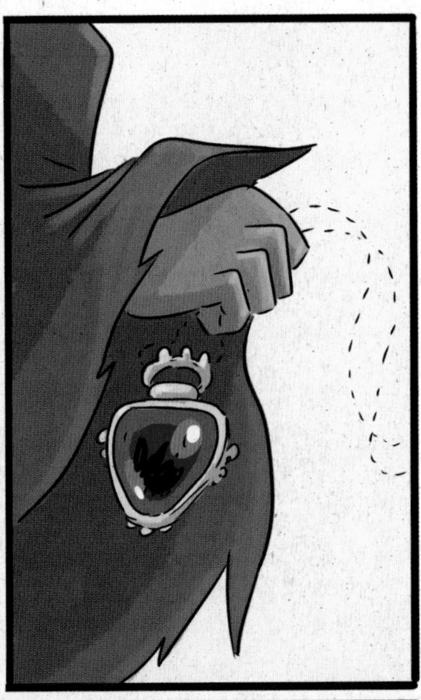

Wait!

That's mine!

POP!

Let... go!
No!

Ahh!

Isabel? Isabel, we're almost at the station.

Excuse me. Have you seen a...? Never mind.

You're human?

I thought humans can't be on this side of the Veil.
They can't.

Well, *he* can!
Stop!

Isabel! Wait!
Ouf!

Heh... Wrong door.

What are *you?*

Guards! Arrest the humans!

Great, this is just what I need.

Chn
Chn Chn
FSSHH

Get back here!
Head back to the other car!
No.
Crrnch!
Snapp!

Ergh!!

That kid's run away from guards before!
What do you think you're doing?

If this is how he did it--

--it's how we'll do it, too.

Grab those two!
He's up ahead!
I think it's time we shake a leg in a running-like fashion.
We *are* running.
Dang.

A human?!
Stop!
Watch it!
My word!

Button...?

Well, at least the necklace is working for us!

foosh

Ah!!!
Why did you try to steal my necklace?

Stop followin' me! You're gonna get me arrested.
You tried to rob me! I'm not going to feel *bad* for you.
I steal to *live.* It's not like a lot of fairies are looking to adopt a *human* child.

Because humans are supposed to be on your side of the Veil.

She's here! Plus she's got weird powers. Yell at her!
I'm not "she," I'm Isabel and this is Button.

We're on a mission from the Seelie court!
Um, not that it's any of your business.

You're a Seelie agent? Ha! They must be desperate if they're recruiting little kids now.

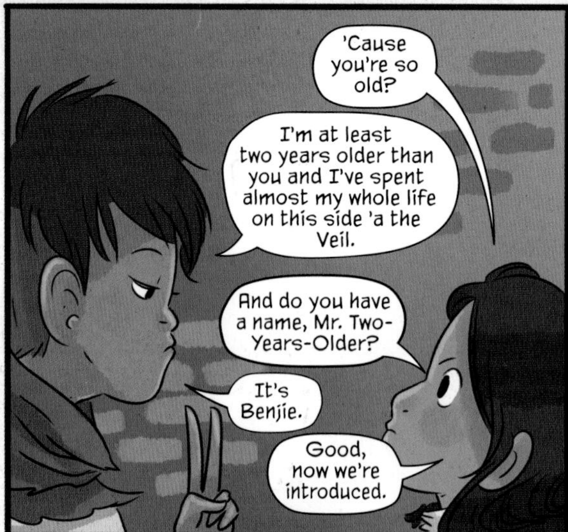
'Cause you're so old?
I'm at least two years older than you and I've spent almost my whole life on this side 'a the Veil.
And do you have a name, Mr. Two-Years-Older?
It's Benjie.
Good, now we're introduced.

How did you get here anyway? Can you move from one side to the other all on your own?

It was the quake...

Not a lot of people made it out of Chinatown. No one seemed to want to save us. And I'm not even Chinese; I'm Filipino.

"When the quake hit, my parents put me in a closet. It was safer."

Help! ***Please!*** Someone!

Skritch Skritch

Who...are you?

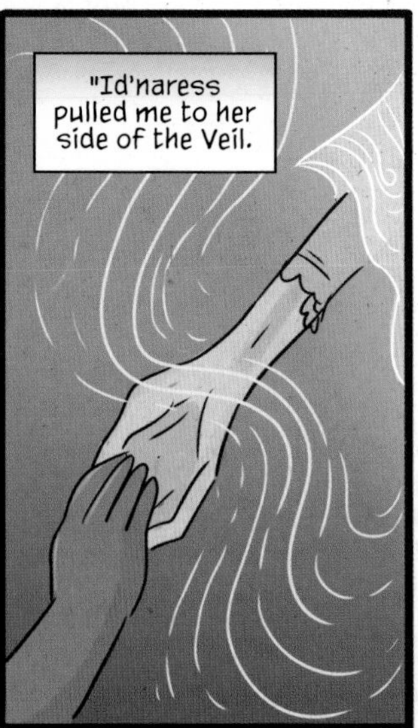
"Id'naress pulled me to her side of the Veil.

"She saved me.
"She said she'd come back for me.

"But she never did. They say she died, like my parents.
"Ever since then I've been able to move back and forth whenever I want."

I just didn't have anything to go back to.

How did you survive?
Stealing, mostly. Fairies are obsessed with stuff that humans don't think twice about.

And don't get high and mighty, fungus.
Losing a bit of ribbon doesn't ruin anyone's life, but it keeps mine going.

So, if Id'naress saved you...will you help us save her? We need to find someone named Miyori.
You don't want me.
I don't have anyone else.

...Fine.

Miyori's a Seelie general in the Unseelie capital, though. You'll never find him.
But someone has to know where he is. Fairies eat... Don't they?

Of course they do. Some a lot more than others. Right, fungus?
Okay, so Miyori needs supplies.

Anyone moving things on the black market needs Frogfoot's permission.
Frogfoot? Never heard of him.

He's a criminal! He's not exactly throwing himself a parade.
Frogfoot is the top boss of the entire city. If anyone knows where Miyori is, he does.

But if he keeps such a low profile, how do we find this Frogfoot exactly?

You've got me, fungus.
Put this on. We don't want to draw a crowd.
Keep your eyes open. I want to know how long we stay on Third Street.
Isabel, I love you like my own sporeling, but this is a limping, half-brained idea if I've ever heard of one. He's a criminal.

Id'naress trusted him.

I don't want to speak ill of the princess, but who knows what she saw in this short-panted huckster.
Follow *my* lead, Isabel. I'll keep you--

Shh!
Stick close, you two. Chinatown isn't always safe. Especially for weirdos like you.

CHO
CHOP
SILKY
店
ALL-WORLD DELICACY
YES WE DO HAVE KRAKEN

RET
FRESH-CAUGHT
書

Wow.
Look at all
the--
I
said to act
normal.

Stop here!
Pretend to be
interested.
Ugh.

You think
standing in the open
won't get us arrested?
How have you **not** been
caught yet?

Wait
for it...
And
then it hits
her...

...right
in her third
eye!
It's not
that funny,
Greg.
Go,
now.

Benjie, how do you know this Frogfoot person?
I told you, Frogfoot runs all the smuggling in the city. I have to sell to *someone.*

Is he Seelie?
Yeah, but he's still a smuggler and not the nicest person.
He's not terrible, I mean... Everything's just been so mixed up since the war started.

Just, don't say anything. Follow my lead and it'll all be fine.

Why is it always everyone else who's leading?

YOU LET THEM ESCAPE?!
We tried to detain them, ma'am, but they had tremendous magic and--

They were just humans, after all.
Humans with "tremendous magic." That didn't strike you as enough to pursue them?
Well... it was odd. But--
Just... quiet.
Coscar doesn't know about this yet. If we act quickly, maybe he won't have to.
Where exactly were they headed?
That way.
Then seal the city. No one gets in or out. And tell every guard you see to...find...that... **GIRL!**

Do you enjoy the hunt, Torrent?

Actually... my race is vegetarian; we don't normally--

I mean, yes! I can't wait to *get* that human.

I'm shaking in my scales. The girl is the priority; she has the necklace, but I want *both* the humans if I can get them.

And the fairy they're traveling with.

Just follow my fin.

Where do you think you're goin', two-arms?
Cho! It's me, Benjie. I'm just here to see Frogfoot.
We remember him. Don't we, Cho?
Right, Wan. We just don't remember *them*.
They're with me.
I also don't remember you being allowed to bring guests.

He'll want to see us. Trust me.

Ha! "Trust me," says the thief.
You trust thieves?
Try not to.

Well, I'm *not* a thief. I'm a ***Seelie agent*** and--
Isabel... quiet.

You will stand aside right now or I'll speak with your supervisor!

Well? I don't like to be kept waiting, gentlemen, and neither does the Seelie court.
Supervisor?
Or should I tell my superiors that Frogfoot wouldn't even hear us out?
Is she serious?
What do I know? I'm just a human.

Profits are down in--

Mr. Frogfoot, sir.

You are not a stupid boy, Benjie. Yet you barge in here unannounced, uninvited, with ***two strangers*** no less.

Tell me why this is. Quickly.

I knew you'd want to hear this.

Mr. Frogfoot, my name is Isabel and I've been given a very important mission by the Seelie court.

We've been sent to find Miyori. We have something for him that could change the tide of the war. And you better help us, or else.

Or what?
Or the Unseelie will win.

If you could help us find Miyori, I know the Seelie would be *forever* grateful.

No.
No?! You damp-brained--
Enough!
You asked me to listen and I have. But all you have given me are obligations to a losing side.
What do I care if the Seelie or Unseelie run things? They both try to shut down my business.
Give me something of value! Not hot air!
Give me something I can...

Now that necklace, *that* clearly has value. What is it, girl?
Nothing, sir.
I know "nothing" when I see it, human. That's not nothing.
It's also not yours!

No disrespect intended, sir. But the necklace is unavailable.

It's part of my mission. It's already promised to someone else.

We're not here to barter, Mr. Frogfoot, and I don't think you really see the Seelie and Unseelie as the same thing.

I hope not; I know the Unseelie hurt people in ways I pray the Seelie never did.

How long until they decide to hurt you, too?

You aren't... entirely wrong. *Disrespectful*, but not wrong.
I'm still not inclined to risk my legs for a Seelie plot...
...but...
...I've heard rumors of Miyori and some Seelie holdouts hiding south of Market Street. Somewhere off Delancey.
If you find him, and actually manage to win this war, remember who--
Sir!
Some Unseelie fish-woman's at the door. She--

Everyone, **FREEZE!**

You can't just barge in here! Mr. Frogfoot is a respected businessman.

One harboring enemies of the Unseelie. How respectable is that?

That's her, ma'am. That's the girl the Seelie messenger gave the necklace to!

I know nothing about that.

A mistake soon remedied--

No!!

Ah!
Urh!

Isabel! Run!

Get back here!

SNP
Rrrh! I'm... stuck!
SNP

You can't escape from me, girl.

Let go of me!
No!
POP!
Come back--

--here!
huff, huff

Benjie? Button?

<Who are you? What are you doing in my house?>*
Huh?
*Translated from Cantonese

<GET OUT!>
I'm sorry! I--

<Thief! That little hoodlum tried to rob me!>

Slow down! You're going to hurt someone!

Where am I? Was that Clay Street?
What's that near?

She made it. Attagirl.

Your concern is touching.

But I'd worry more about myself right now, Seelie.
If he even *starts* to fade, gut him. We'll see how fast his magic works then.
Now...Mr. Frogfoot? Convince me you aren't a traitor to the Unseelie and I *shouldn't* have you very swiftly executed.
SNAP!
I am a business-fairy, my lady. Nothing more.
Do what you want with the mushroom and boy.
I'd hate for anyone to think Frogfoot was... unhelpful...to the authorities.
So would I.

What do you think? Should we just ask them where their friends disappeared to?
I say we punch the answers out of them.

Well, I don't favor brutality myself. I'm sure you're both eager to cooperate--

We're not going to tell you a root-twisted thing!

Because we don't know anything.

Really? You're just respectable businessfairies, too?

Of course not, we're thieves.

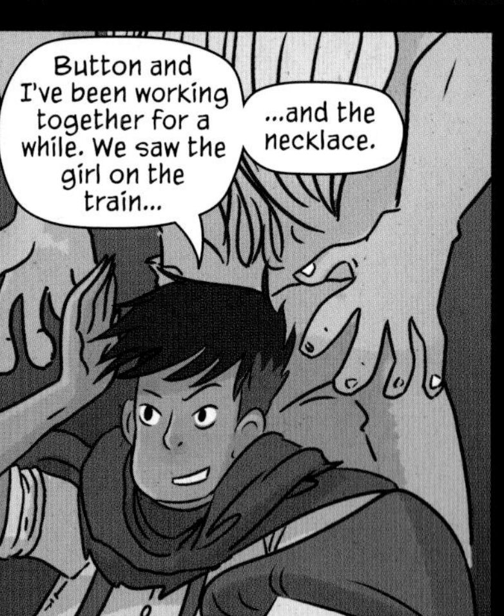
Button and I've been working together for a while. We saw the girl on the train...
...and the necklace.

And you knew its value?

I knew it was shiny and she was little.
We brought her here to fleece her.

The mush-room told her to run.
He's a little greedy. Didn't want to split it. But we want cash, not trouble.

Very well.
Spine! They're lying!
How do you know?
I saw the fungi with the girl...I think... I'm **almost** positive.
Probably true, but hardly enough. I will not have it said that the Unseelie are unjust.
Return to the palace. Perhaps the prince's oracles will be able to find this girl.

You have brought a lot of trouble to my door, boy.
But I know how you can make it up to me.
If Coscar wants that necklace, I want that necklace.
His oracles will never find her before she gets to Miyori... but you can.
Bring me that necklace, or neither of you will ever be safe on this side of the Veil again.

And just so you don't forget your priorities...
We'll keep your companion.
Unhand me!
I get it, sir. But if you want that necklace, I need the fungus.
I'd never help you steal from the Seelie, or betray Isabel!
He doesn't seem very inclined to help.
He will be.

I'm not close enough to Isabel to get her trust back, not on my own.
But, together, she won't suspect a thing.
Because she trusts us! You slick-fingered thief!
I know where you got on that train. If you don't help me, I'm gonna go back to that stop and tell the Unseelie to burn it to the ground.
But it doesn't have to be that way.
I *remember* the people who help me. I'd do *anything* to help them in return.
I...
...I'll help.

Fine. You can both bring me the necklace.
And be quick!

Didn't you hear what I was saying?
You said you'd hurt Isabel and burn down my house.

I said I remember people who helped me.

I had to make them *think* I was with them to free you.
I'm not a very big fairy, or a strong one, or a fast one.

But I told Isabel I'd get her and that necklace to Miyori. Do you remember that?
Yeah. So let's do it together.

How do I know I can trust you?
That's not how trust works, Button.
You either trust me or you don't. So, what do you say?

Frogfoot's never gonna let you come back without the necklace.
It's not about the necklace. It's about helping Isabel.

Okay then...let's help her.

Good man!
I won't let you down.
I promise...
What did I tell you?

Why torture people for information you can't rely on, when just following them leads to so much better results?
Brilliant, ma'am.

But what if they go to the other side of the Veil? We can't follow there.

"Neither can the mushroom spirit.

"Even if the human leaves.

"They'll have to come back.
"See?"

Let's get 'em.
Patience, Torrent.
Patience. We need the necklace, but if we get Miyori as well, it will end the Seelie in one stroke.
You're okay!
Of course, kiddo. I'm me, after all.
I knew we could count on you.
Yeah, me, too.
Eventually...

Now we just need to find Miyori...
Which puts us back at square one. Right where we were before we met you, Benjie.

But I got you a clue. Give me your map, Isabel.

Frogfoot said the warehouse was somewhere near Delancey. I know that area. It's full of warehouses; it should be dead at night.

We just have to find whatever warehouse isn't.

Why is everything still so damaged? It's not like this on the human side of the Veil.
It got hit hard during the war. The Unseelie wanted to cut off Seelie supplies from the piers.

We have to keep our eyes peeled for anything suspicious.

Like him?
I don't know, Isabel...

...I don't think even the Unseelie are desperate enough to recruit that guy.
BEST PRICES
PAWN

Have you seen any bars here? Any liquor stores?
No.

Not a lot of customers to keep that pawn shop busy right now, either.

Let's figure out why he's watching it so closely.

SQUA!

KSSH!

RAID!

CHNK!
CHNK!
Unseelie! They've found us!
Get back!
We're not-- Look out!
Ah!
I don't want to hurt you! I can't control it!

Oof!
Argh!
I know that magic.

Where did you acquire that necklace?
It is not *for* you!
Give it to me!
It's mine! I won't let anyone take it!

I was not *asking*.
No! I made a promise!

I'm supposed to--

--give it to--

...
Miyori?

Yes, my lady?
What news from the front, Miyori?
Wait...

...he's Miyori?
It is unsettling. Prince Coscar's forces gain strength and may attack the city any day now.

I fear we may not be able to hold the city.
Have faith.
This...is someone's memory.

Faith? If I may speak plainly. I fear for your safety, dear heart.

We have to get you out of here before it's too late.

You're Miyori! You were there!
Where? Have you been watching me?!

Spies for the Unseelie, that's what you are.
No! I mean... I saw it, just now. My necklace showed it to me.
You were talking to someone. You were worried about her safety. You called her "dear heart."
I--I called Id'naress that when she was small. And once more, the last time I saw her.
No one else was there. No one could know that.
My necklace did.
The Seelie took it from Coscar and gave it to me. I promised them I'd give it to you.

It can do more than that. It's how I was able to control the room. The whole city seems to respond to it.

And the Seelie who gave it to you said to bring it to me?

Why? Who are you?

My name's Isabel. She didn't want to give me the necklace.

I mean, she wanted to bring it herself, but...she didn't make it.

You are a very brave child.

Was Id'naress brave?

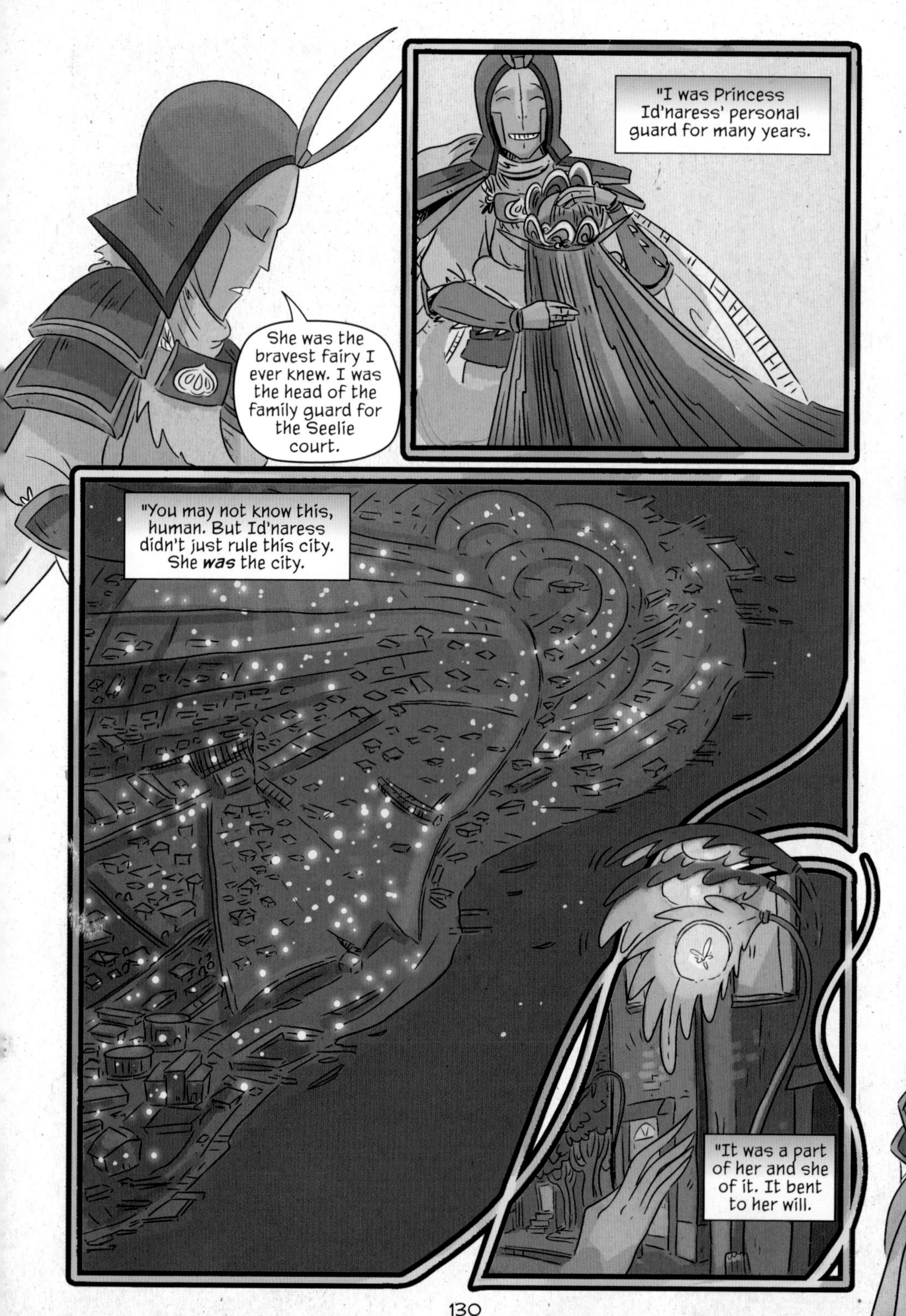
"I was Princess Id'naress' personal guard for many years.
She was the bravest fairy I ever knew. I was the head of the family guard for the Seelie court.
"You may not know this, human. But Id'naress didn't just rule this city. She *was* the city.
"It was a part of her and she of it. It bent to her will.

"And when she went missing, when Prince Coscar *stole* her, he gained that power, too."
And now *you* have it.
The necklace and her powers, both.
Which means that necklace is somehow tied to Id'naress herself.

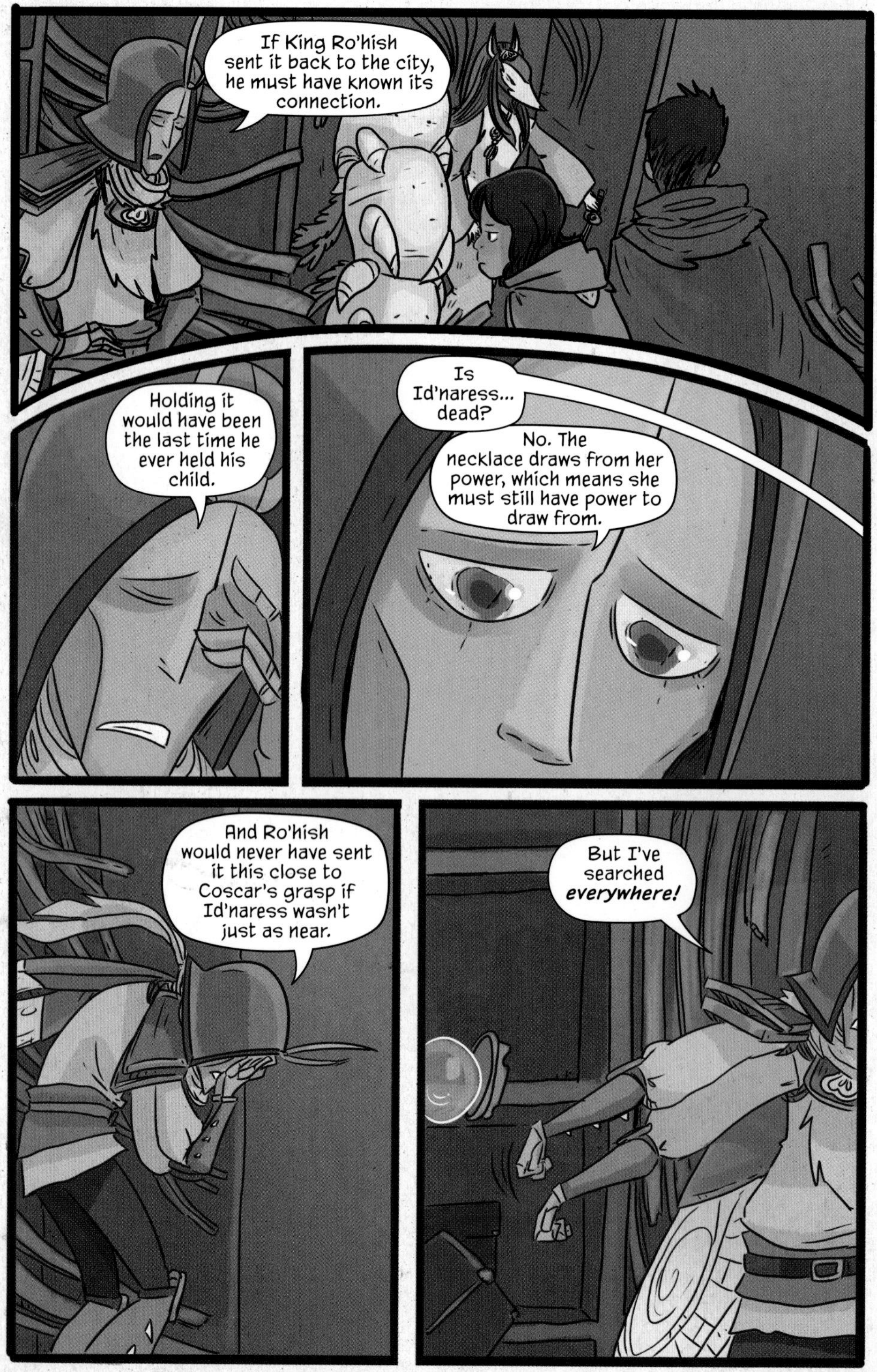

If King Ro'hish sent it back to the city, he must have known its connection.

Holding it would have been the last time he ever held his child.

Is Id'naress... dead?

No. The necklace draws from her power, which means she must still have power to draw from.

And Ro'hish would never have sent it this close to Coscar's grasp if Id'naress wasn't just as near.

But I've searched *everywhere!*

Well *we* haven't. We'll find her, Miyori. I promise.
I wouldn't do that.
After all, you're only as good as your word.

My thanks for leading me here, human, but Frogfoot won't be getting that necklace...
...Prince Coscar will.

Benjie--?

Stay behind me, Isabel. No Unseelie is going to touch you.
The war's already over, Miyori. Your king is dead. His fortress is ours.

Just give us the necklace and we can finally bury this conflict.

Never!

Are you just looking to die in battle, general?

I am looking to win.

Miyori, sir! You must retreat!
Miyori!
GAH!
No! The children are the priority.

Then take them!
Go!
I'll handle these grubby yellow-bellies. Once a Seelie soldier, always a Seelie soldier.
Button! No!
Coward!
KRRRECCHHHH!

Take the others into custody! Miyori is mine!
THK

Come on, you three-legged dogs!
I'll take you all on myself!
AHHH!
BES
PA
TRN-SKREE CKSSH!
Don't look back, girl. The road ahead is too long for that.

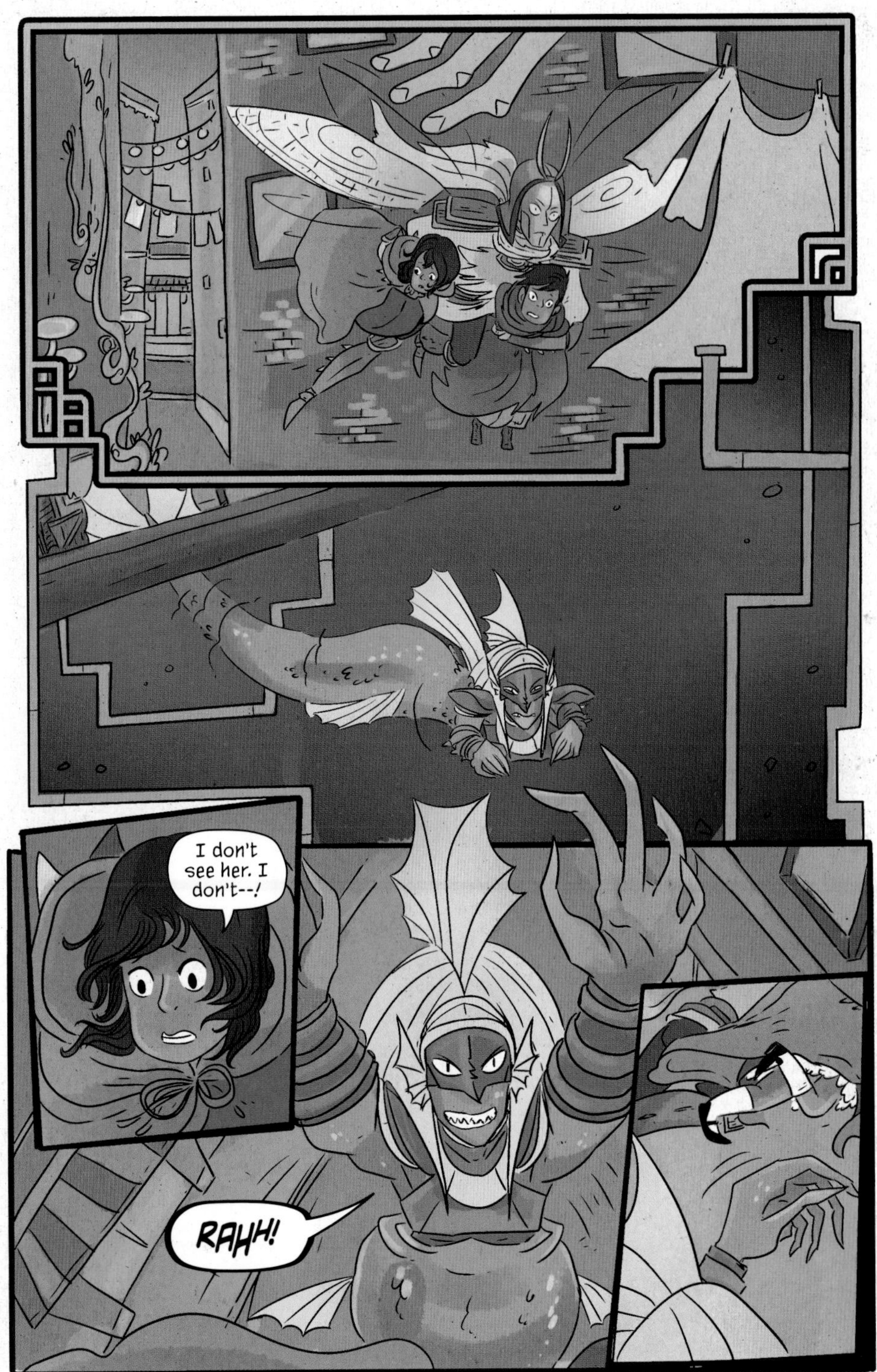
I don't see her. I don't--!
RAHH!

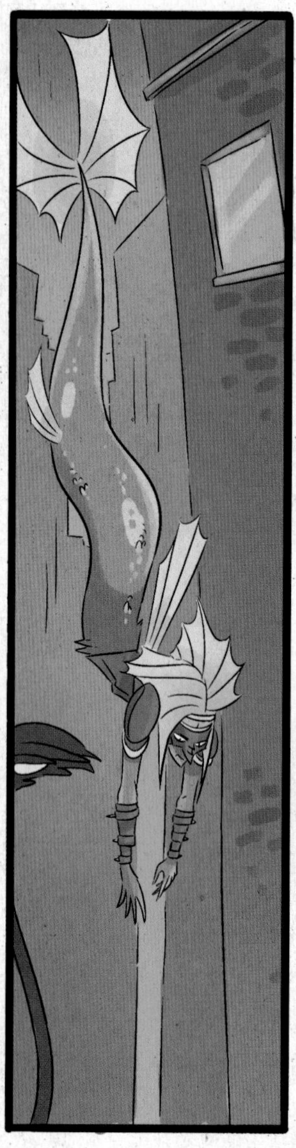
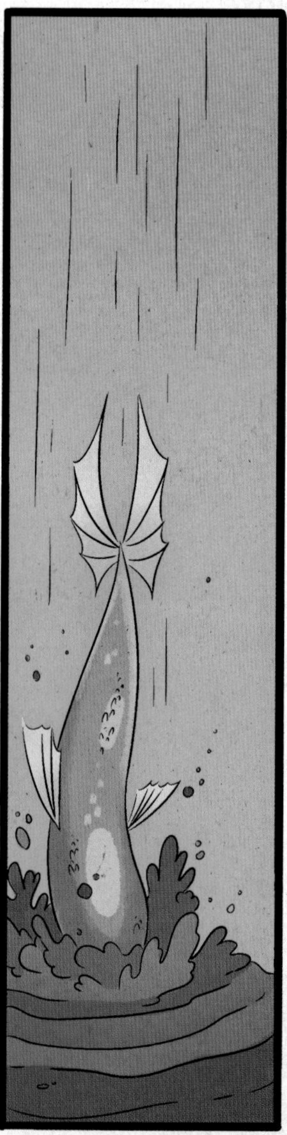

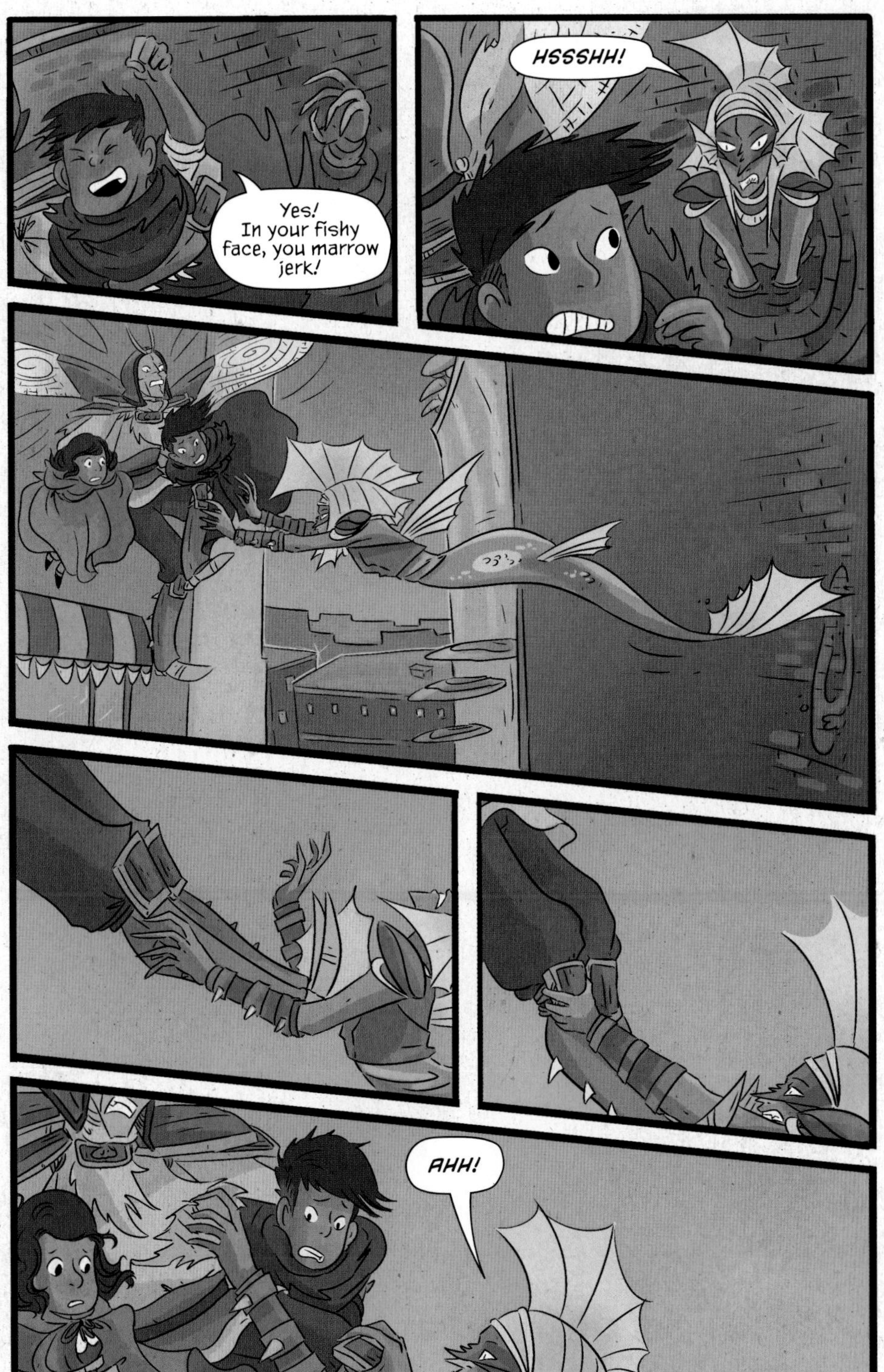
Yes! In your fishy face, you marrow jerk!
HSSSHH!
AHH!

Let us go!
Please!

Hang on!

KRRCH!

...Run.

Let's see how you like being underfoot, Seelie.

RUN!

Oww.

Isabel... we've gotta go.
Benjie...

Benjie, I'm hurt.

Help me.
"Bring me that necklace, or neither of you will ever be safe on this side of the Veil again."

I'm sorry.

What?

Benjie... Let go.
It's over, Isabel. We can't win.
At least this way we can survive.

Stop it!

...

Look out!

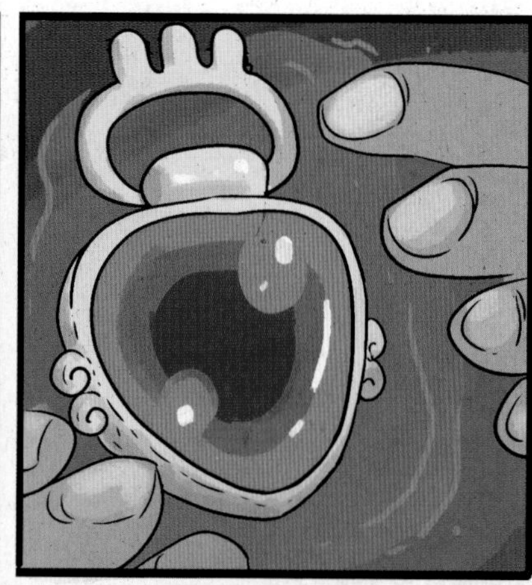

Rahh!

Rrrrrr...

huff...
huff...
HNNNK!
HNNK!

Outta the road, ya stupid kids!

No matter what.

Isabel,
I'm sorry.

Frogfoot wanted the necklace and...I can't hide from him forever. I--
I know how to be a thief.

I don't want to be one but maybe I'm just a bad kid. Maybe that's why the quake took my mom and dad.

Benjie...

Don't ever think that.

You're not the only one that grownups think they can push around.
With those clothes? Your parents musta loved you.
Maybe, but Mother never said it.

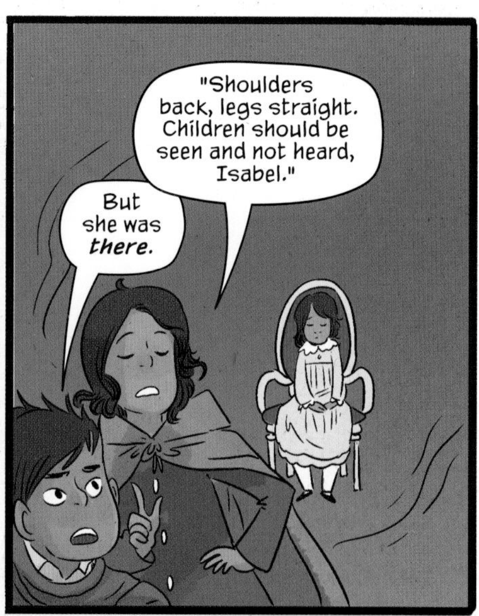
"Shoulders back, legs straight. Children should be seen and not heard, Isabel."
But she was *there*.

"That was the problem. She was *just there*. And she wanted me to be *just there*, too.

"Maybe it wasn't as bad. I wasn't hungry. I had a bed."

Isabel?

Mary!

Take care of her, please. We talked about this.

"But I always felt...in the way."

Sweetheart, you know better than to interrupt. Did you have a bad dream?
...I just wanted to say good night.
"Even Papa doesn't want me, not really."

No one thinks I can *do anything.* No one *cares* as long as I don't mess up my dress.

And no one cares what *you* want to do, either, as long as you give them what they want.

But *they're* wrong, not *us.* We're not worthless or useless.

Id'naress saw that, Benjie. She saved you.
Now she needs someone to save her!

Don't you at least want to try?

We don't exactly look very ***heroic***, you know.
Of course not.
That's so we can strike where they least suspect.

Um, Isabel?
How are we gonna
find her?
...

Miyori looked for Id'naress for months and didn't find anything.

Whole armies have looked for her. Even Frogfoot sent people out once.
How are we gonna find her when the entire fairy world can't?

I've been thinking about that.

You're right; the fairies have looked everywhere they can. But there isn't just one world, there's two because of the Veil.

You and I can move across it thanks to Id'naress' magic.
And Coscar is just as strong; he's her counterpart.
Exactly!

So what if he hid her where no other fairy could look?
This side of the Veil!

Isabel! You're a genius!

We just have to figure out where she is in this version of the city and free her!

It's still a pretty big place. I don't even know what Id'naress looks like.

She looked like...like part of the city come to life.
She had blue-gray skin, like fog. Long, pointed ears. Her hair was like wires and she wore a crown shaped like a bunch of--

--waves.

Yeah, how did you know?
Because I've seen her before, Benjie!

There was a picture of her in the newspaper...I put it in my map and I-- I don't have my map!

It must have fallen out in the fight!
Yes. But I don't have any money.
It's okay. Was the newspaper recent?
I know a place.

CLLNG!

I'VE GOT IT!
Isabel, keep it down!

Hey! You kids get outta there!
Benjie?
Oh, great. Now we've gotta run.

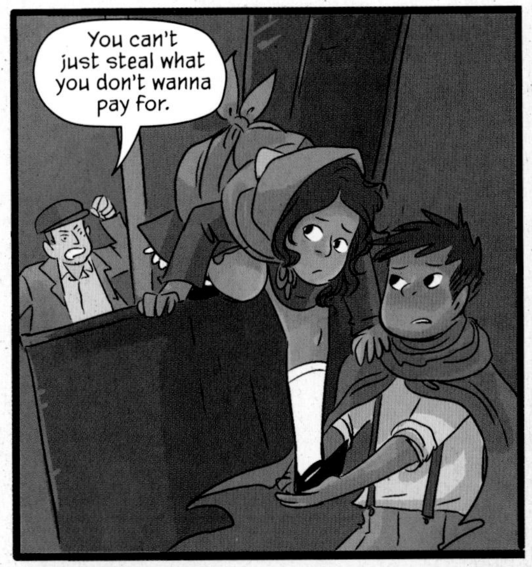
You can't just steal what you don't wanna pay for.

Relax! It's literally old news!

Do you think he's following us?
Nah. He can't exactly get too far from his stand or someone might steal his ***actual*** merchandise, not his trash.

So, what did you find?
An ad for a new art exhibit at the de Young Museum. See who's there?

That's her. It's Id'naress!
I knew it! The museum's in Golden Gate Park. It's just west of here. Follow me!

CALIFORNIA STREET
How do you know so much about the city? I thought you were always locked up.
LONE MT.
I was, but I still loved the city.
3
DE YOUNG MUSEUM
BUENA VISTA PARK
TWIN PEAKS
4
I love the fog and the bay and all the alleys that dead-end someplace new. And just because I wasn't there, doesn't mean I can't imagine it.
MISS

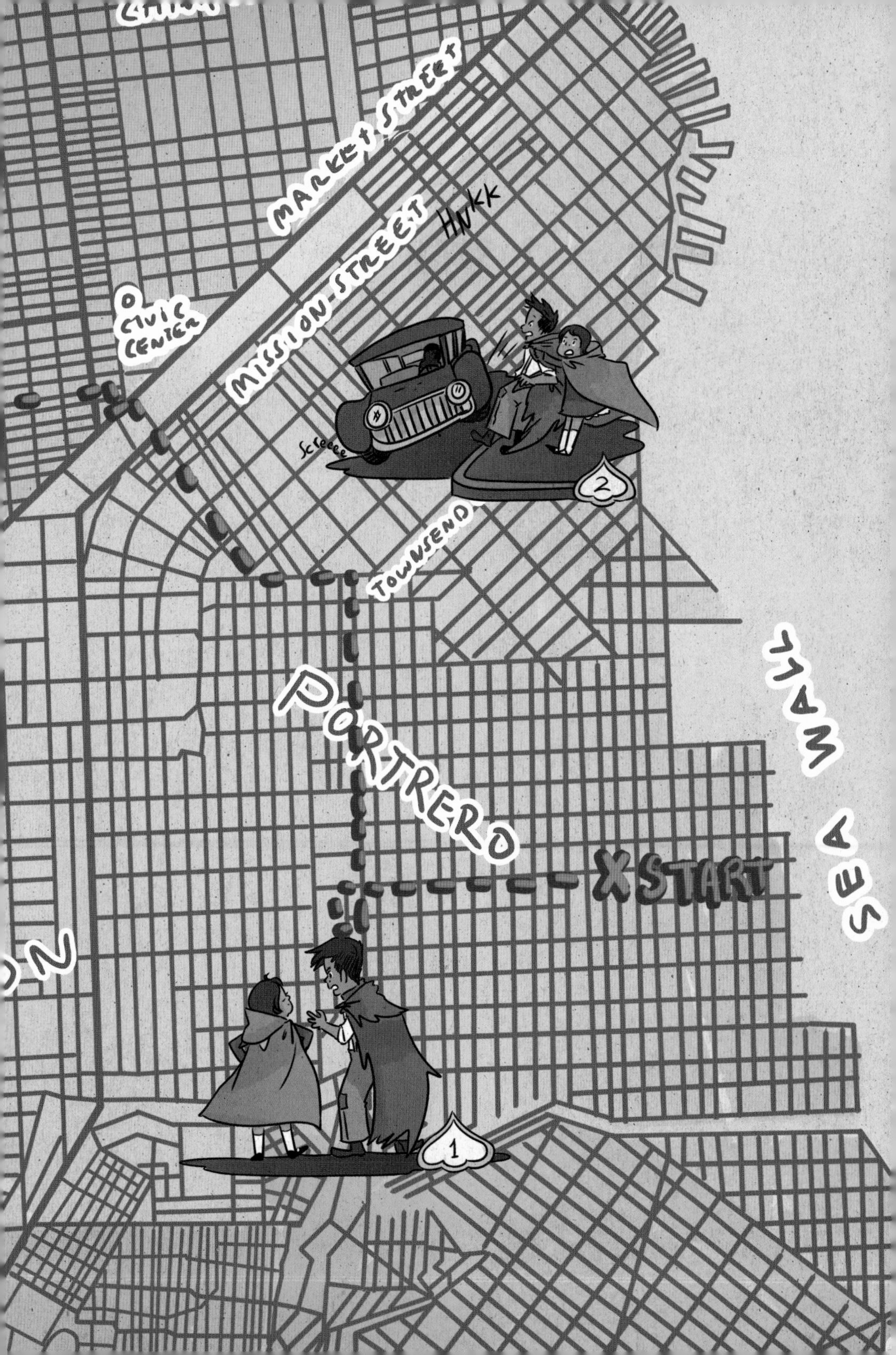

MARKET STREET
MISSION STREET
HNKK
CIVIC CENTER
Screeee
2
TOWNSEND
PORTRERO
XSTART
SEA WALL
1

It's just... it was all on the other side of a different Veil. The one my mom made.
Well, welcome to San Francisco, Isabel.

We're here.
Oh, no.

What?
On the other side of the Veil...

"...this is Coscar's palace."

"We can't break in
on the other side.
No way."

Well, then we'll just have to break in ***on this side*** of the Veil.
Have you ever broken into a place before?

Benjie, everything in my house is locked all the time.

Just help me up.

There's no window, Isabel.

Isabel...
whatever
you're gonna
do--hurry!

Open...
please?

Thank
you.

Wow, you are getting really good at this.
The necklace is getting stronger, too.
We're definitely getting close.
I'm pretty sure it's this way.
Watch out!

Is someone there?

Huh. Must be more tired than I thought.

Phew.
NEW EXHIBIT! LADY OF THE CITY

...he fought valiantly, but in vain. And for a trinket.
It's more than a--

Wait...do you sense that?

The necklace... it's close.
Find it!

Scour the palace!

I don't get it; how was Coscar able to keep Id'naress imprisoned for so long if they're equally strong?
Fairies hate metal, especially cold iron. They can't even touch it without being hurt.
If Coscar imprisoned Id'naress in cold iron, she'd never escape.

But if fairies can't touch cold iron, how can Id'naress be inside it and still be alive?

Painfully. Very painfully.

LADY of the CITY

NO!

Ah!

Urgh.
Isabel!

You defile my castle, my realm, with your very presence. You defy my will at every turn.

This is not your war, human. This is not your world.

Return my necklace and I'll return you to your side of the Veil.
Let no one say Coscar is without mercy.

You didn't show ***any*** mercy to Id'naress. You imprisoned her in a way that would make her suffer.

You stole her heart and hid it.

You are not a fairy! You know nothing of the plight of the Unseelie.
I know Id'naress cared about this city. She helped us when she didn't have to.

She helped herself!
You humans think whatever benefits you benefits all...
No, that's not it...
You don't think beyond yourselves *AT ALL!*
He's right!
Disgusting humans!
You're the real reason this war started. Humans destroyed our people's balance, ***not me.***

The Seelie have always been cunning. They saw the greed in Humanity and harnessed it to their own ends.
"Every human Id'naress helped increased her power.
"Never mind the fairies who were cut down and paved over.
"Well, I am the spirit of the rock itself.
"Am I supposed to lie still with Humanity crushing my back--binding *me* to *their* will?
"She thought so!"

Why shouldn't Id'naress let me rule half the year? Every year my power diminished as hers grew.
The Seelie sat back and allowed the Unseelie to be destroyed *for* them.
I had to attack first! There was no other way!
So you caused the earthquake?
How was killing us any better than what you say we did to you?
Your judgment means nothing to me, boy.
As long as one human remains, no Unseelie will be safe.

You must all be destroyed.

Now give me the necklace!

You can't have it!

SHNG

Last chance, girl. Give it to me or be destroyed!

Isabel! Run!

Is that all you've got, old man?

No.

Ahh!

But it would appear that's all *you* have, child.

You've just lost your war.

O-O-O-O-•

Coscar! Get back!
This is--
--between--
Urgh!
--you--
--and me.

You've already lost, Id'naress. The only thing useful about you now is your jewelry.
Ruling is not about finding a use for others, Coscar. It is about making yourself useful *to them*.
But you've never been able to see that.
And now you never will.

HAAH!
TNK

Help me, you fools!

But you said Id'naress had run away.
And *you* ordered us not to interfere, ***sir***.

Fine. I'll do it myself, as I ***always*** have.

I defeated you once; I can do it again.
No, Coscar. You cannot. Because I see you this time.
It's time to return to your home, stone spirit. Rumble all you like from there.
Coscar, I reject you as my equal. I deny you are my shadow. I refuse you in all things.

NOOOOOO!

Your prince is defeated. Your war against us is lost. If you would fight me, do it now and you can join him.

Id'naress, don't blame them for your imprisonment. Coscar said you ran. We didn't know you were here.

Blame me. I was his captain.
Whatever punishment you choose, I will *not* run from my fate.

Your life is not what I desire, Unseelie.

This war was not my desire, either. I only wanted peace.

I cannot do that without you.

There cannot be Seelie without Unseelie, and I cannot be without a counterpart.

You must choose a new leader.

I hope you pick someone who will heal our wounds.

But it is your choice.

Spine.

It should be Spine. She's led us and she offered her life for ours.

Spine!
Spine!
Spine!
Spine!
Spine!

I... accept.
Then I agree.
Spine of the Marrow, I see you as my equal.

"I name you my
dark reflection.
"I honor you and hold
you close in the light
of the noonday sun.
"I honor you and beg
your comfort in the
darkness of the
moonless night."
My comfort is
yours, Id'naress.
As I, Spine, rule
the Unseelie, you
will be held safe
throughout the
night.

For we are one as all things are.

Seelie and Unseelie together.

Coscar was wrong to wage this war, for no balance can be achieved in extermination.
But I will also not abandon my people to a quiet destruction.

Nor would I see them go. Let this war prove only that we must stand together, or ***both*** be destroyed.

Though without both of you, *I* would have been destroyed.
Id'naress, Benjie is--

Do not fear, Isabel. He is easily healed.
Uhh...

Uh... Thank you.

They fought well for you, Id'naress. They refused to give up. They are truly heroes.

I'm not really a hero.

Why not? Because you stumbled from the righteous path?

I was there, Benjie. I felt everything that happened while my heart was taken from me.

And I remember the little boy I pulled from the rubble. I will not leave him again.

I name you a ward of the Seelie. Our world will not survive without insight into Humanity. If you will give us that, I will shelter you for all of your days.

You have my thanks and my love.

Thank you.

And so was the end of the last Cold Iron War.

Button! Are you alright?

You shoulda seen me, kiddo. I gave those curs what-for!

Spine reunited Button with Isabel.

Id'naress escorted them both home in the lap of luxury.

Not realizing that home was the last place Isabel wanted to go.

The others are gonna drop their jaws, Isabel! They all missed the chance to have a real adventure!

Isabel, what's wrong?

Nothing, it was a great adventure. I just...

I'm sure Papa didn't even notice I was gone.

Let us see what your father is actually doing.

...and you're sure Isabel hasn't been there?

No. I can't reach her mother.
Thank you anyway.

He's been on the phone since you left, trying to find you. He searched for miles, went to the police. This is all he can do now, so he does it.

He wasn't interested in me when I was there.

And you did not rush to see ***him*** when you came back. Do you not love your father?
No! I mean, I ***do.*** I--I'm just scared.

Perhaps your father kept his distance because he is scared, too.

You have fought so bravely to find your voice, Isabel. Wouldn't you like your father to hear it?

Hello?
Angelina...

I...
I'm sorry,
I'll...

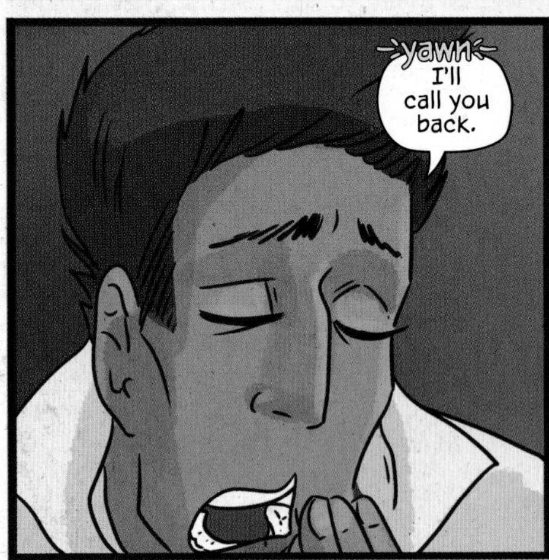
yawn
I'll
call you
back.

...can't
sleep...Isabel
is...

...counting...
on...

Papa?

Isabel!

I'm sorry, I--
I didn't think you would notice.

Princesa... *I'm* sorry.

I know how to work stone, and it was easier to do what I know than what I don't.

But stone cannot replace a daughter.

The rest of the summer proved him right.
It wasn't easy.

But what they made, they made together.

And by working together, even their stumbles weren't so bad.
THE BLUE FAIRY

And when the summer ended, it was hard for Isabel to leave.

Fortunately, this time she didn't have to.

Not really.

I'll visit this weekend. Okay? Be good for your mother.
I will.

Miss Isabel. I'm terribly sorry, your mother is delayed and--
No problem! Good-bye, Papa!

Now, instead of having no home, she had two.
I'll be in my room!

One in the country...
We're here! We're home!

...and one in the city.
Ready to go?
Always.
Just not the city you know.

The End

I hope you enjoyed *The City on the Other Side.*
Actually, I'm *sure* you did.
I'm so sure, in fact, that I've made a little treat for those of you who want to learn more about this book and the world inside it.

Button Knows Everything

Ta-da!

A lot of research went into making this book.
There actually was a terrible earthquake in San Francisco in the year 1906. It was so big it was felt from Los Angeles to Oregon!

Large portions of the city were leveled, both by the quake itself and the fires that came afterward.

The city took years to rebuild, and once they finished in 1915, they threw a party you might also have heard of: the Panama-Pacific International Exposition.
Or ***San Francisco's World's Fair***.
Our book is set some time between the fire and the fair.
We don't say exactly when, though. Even fairies don't like to admit their age.
SAN FRANCISCO WORLD'S FAIR
1915

San Francisco is a city with a rich and diverse history.
There have been people living in this region since 3000 BCE.

San Francisco has been claimed by many.

The Spaniards took it from the Ohlone people. Then it passed to Mexico, and was finally taken by the United States.

When the Gold Rush hit in the 1840s, the city grew from a small settlement to a large metropolis.

It also became a major port for trade with Asia.

Many families like Benjie's came from China, the Philippines, and other countries to live here.

So it's always been a diverse city.

And our story reflects that in our fairies as well as our humans.

The fairies in this book were inspired by various different traditions and ideas.
Mythological creatures.
I am a spiritus loci-- a type of Roman spirit that inhabits and embodies a specific place.
I'm a kind of Scottish spirit called a wulver. We're a little like werewolves, but a lot nicer.
We jiangshi are fabled undead from China who get around by hopping from place to place.
Spirits of California plants.
I'm the spirit of a redbud, Cercis occidentalis.
I'm based on a western morning glory, Calystegia occidentalis.
And a few of us are just fun.
To see how some of us evolved, turn the page and find the first sketches Robin ever drew of our main characters! Enjoy!
And... well, everyone else.
Some of us are designed to show a period of more ancient history.
And some of us show off how things looked in our "modern day."

Isabel's Disguise
OR Why Mairghread doesn't draw her own books

ISABEL

BENJIE

BUTTON

SPINE

Thanks to Jason, my everything.

—*M.S.*

Thanks to Steph and Elle for being my gracious guides to The City and its history, to CJ and ALK for keeping me sane through deadlines, my parents for the childhood visiting artists in the Bay Area, and NHR, who knows what he did.

—*R.R.*

MAIRGHREAD SCOTT is an animation and comic book writer specializing in action-comedy. Her animation work spans such titles as *Guardians of the Galaxy*, *Ultimate Spider-Man*, *Transformers: Robots in Disguise*, and more. You can also read her work in comic book series such as: *Marvel Universe Guardians of the Galaxy*, *Transformers: Till All Are One*, *Wonder Woman 75th Anniversary Special*, and her creator-owned work *Toil and Trouble*. She is the author of the graphic novel *Science Comics: Robots & Drones*, also from First Second.

ROBIN ROBINSON draws books for both kids and adults, and has always identified with the ghosts and fairies and monsters in stories. With a background in game art as well as picture book illustration and a lifelong love of comics and animation, she has found a way to artistically nerd out in all her favorite media. Robin tries to live every day like it's Halloween.

EXPLORE NEW WORLDS WITH :01

First Second
www.firstsecondbooks.com

Foiled
by Jane Yolen and Mike Cavallaro
"An enchanting tale."
—*Kirkus Reviews*

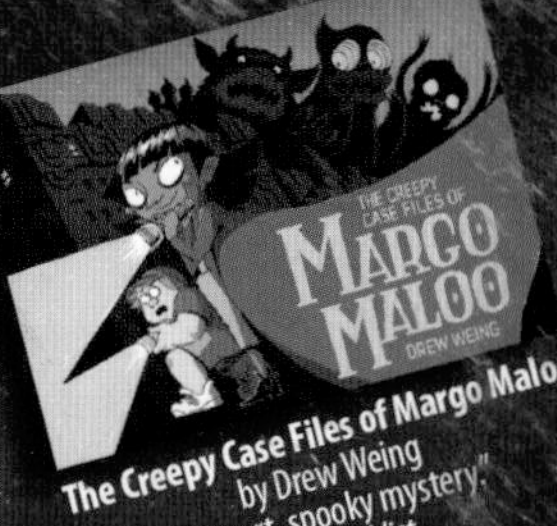

The Creepy Case Files of Margo Maloo
by Drew Weing
"Smart, spooky mystery."
—*Booklist*

The Time Museum
by Matthew Loux
"Fresh, fast, and funny."
—*Kirkus Reviews* ★

Star Scouts
by Mike Lawrence
"Exciting, laugh-a-minute."
—*Publishers Weekly* ★

The Nameless City
by Faith Erin Hicks
"Breathtaking."
—*New York Times*

Astronaut Academy
by Dave Roman
"Involved and complex comedy."
—*Booklist*

Robot Dreams
by Sara Varon
"Tender, funny, and wise."
—*Publishers Weekly* ★

Giants Beware!
by Jorge Aguirre and Rafael Rosado
"Rollicking fun story."
—*New York Times*

The Unsinkable Walker Bean
by Aaron Renier
"Rip-roaring adventure."
—*Booklist* ★

Zita the Spacegirl
by Ben Hatke
"Adventurous, exciting, funny, and moving."
—*ICV2*

Battling Boy
by Paul Pope
"Dazzling."
—*New York Times*

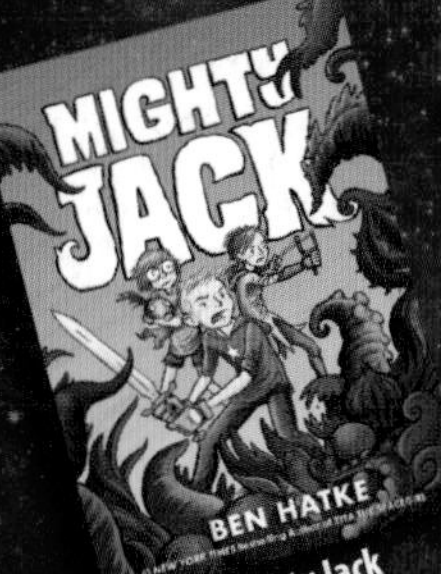

Mighty Jack
by Ben Hatke
"Very mighty indeed."
—*Kirkus Reviews* ★

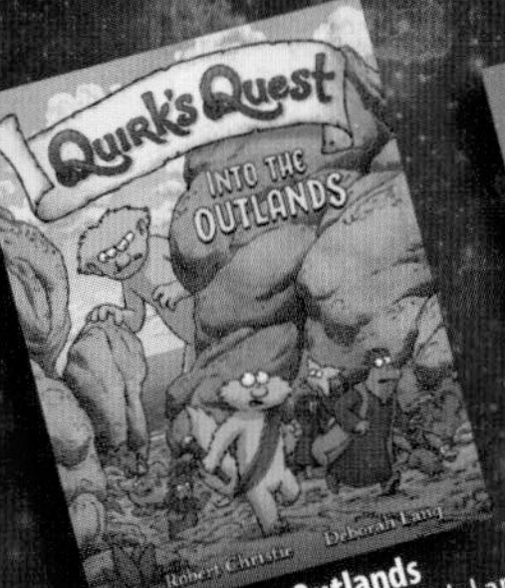

Into the Outlands
by Robert Christie and Deborah Lang
"Full of action, humor, and twists."
—*School Library Journal*

Bera the One-Headed Troll
by Eric Orchard
"Gorgeous."
—*Bulletin of the Center for Children's Books* ★

Published by First Second
First Second is an imprint of Roaring Brook Press,
a division of Holtzbrinck Publishing Holdings Limited Partnership
175 Fifth Avenue, New York, NY 10010

Library of Congress Control Number: 2017941171

Hardcover ISBN: 978-1-250-15255-8
Paperback ISBN: 978-1-62672-457-0

Our books may be purchased in bulk for promotional, educational, or business use.
Please contact your local bookseller or the Macmillan Corporate and Premium Sales Department
at (800) 221-7945 ext. 5442 or by e-mail at MacmillanSpecialMarkets@macmillan.com.

First edition, 2018
Book design by Andrew Arnold, Eileen Gilshian, and Rob Steen
Lettering by Warren Montgomery
Printed in China by1010 Printing International Limited, North Point, Hong Kong

Penciled in Photoshop, inked with Frenden's "The Natural" brush in Manga Studio,
and colored in Photoshop with Robin Robinson's own brushes and textures.

1 3 5 7 9 10 8 6 4 2